Yum
yum

The illustrations for this book were done in wax colors, watercolor pencils, acrylics, and pencil in collage on card stock, also using photo and digital media. The text was set in MetaPro. • Copyright © 2018 by Anna Llenas • English translation copyright © 2020 by Hachette Book Group, Inc. • Cover illustration copyright © 2018 by Anna Llenas. Cover design by Lynn El-Roeiy • Cover copyright © 2020 by Hachette Book Group, Inc. • Hachette Book Group supports the right to free expression and the value of copyright. The purpose of copyright is to encourage writers and artists to produce the creative works that enrich our culture. • The scanning, uploading, and distribution of this book without permission is a theft of the author's intellectual property. If you would like permission to use material from the book (other than for review purposes), please contact permissions@hbgusa.com. Thank you for your support of the author's rights. • Little, Brown and Company • Hachette Book Group • 1290 Avenue of the Americas, New York, NY 10104 • Visit us at LBYR.com • Originally published in 2018 by Editorial Flamboyant in Spain in the Spanish language under the original title *El monstre de colors va a l'escola* • First U.S. Edition: July 2020 • Little, Brown and Company is a division of Hachette Book Group, Inc. • The Little, Brown name and logo are trademarks of Hachette Book Group, Inc. • The publisher is not responsible for websites (or their content) that are not owned by the publisher. • ISBNs: 978-0-316-53704-9 (hardcover), 978-0-316-53707-0 (ebook), 978-0-316-53702-5 (ebook), 978-0-316-53703-2 (ebook) • Printed in Singapore • 10 9 8 7 6 5 4 3 2 1

THE COLOR MONSTER GOES TO SCHOOL

ANNA LLENAS

LB

LITTLE, BROWN AND COMPANY

NEW YORK BOSTON

"Hello, Monster!

I have something exciting to tell you.
Today is your first day at school."

"But what is this thing you call **school**?

A dangerous place full of fierce animals?

A magic cloud in the sky?

A scary forest of traps?"

"Here's your backpack.
You can put everything you need in it."

Helmet

Boots for quicksand

Anti-alien goggles

Flashlight

Bat repellent

Laser
(just in case)

"Why are you bringing all these silly things, Monster?
You just need your smock and a notebook!"

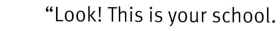

"Look! This is your school.
We're going to have a really good time, Monster.
This is your teacher, Ms. Teresa."

"And this is our classroom.
Now, where have you gone?"

"Let me introduce you to our classmates."

Nuna

Lucas

Tula

Max

Martín

We have music class in the morning.
"You're doing great, Monster!
You're just a little out of tune."

Then Ms. Teresa reads us a story.
"Monster, I can see you *really* like stories."

Later, we head outside to the playground.
The Monster finds a swing.
"Hey, Monster! Give us a turn!"

Before lunch, we go to the bathroom and wash our hands.

Splish
splosh

"What are you doing, Monster?!
No! Don't play with the
toilet paper!"

The morning is over, and we're hungry. Thankfully, it's lunchtime!
"Look, Monster—it's your favorite, alphabet soup and crackers!"

Nooo!

You mustn't play with your food!

With a full tummy, Monster sneaks
into the babies' classroom,
where it's naptime.

Well, they *were* napping....

Grrrrr...
grrrrr...

Good heavens, what loud snoring!

In the afternoon,
we go to the gym for some exercise.

It's so much fun jumping
on the Monster!

Boing…
boing…

We end the day by doing some painting.
We've got the perfect model!

The Monster changes color
when his feelings change.

Say something sweet—

he might turn pink!

School's over and it's time to say goodbye.

It has been a great day.

"School isn't so bad after all.
Are we going again tomorrow?"